D1571652

Scan the QR Code to Access an EXCLUSIVE Reading of the book!

First paperback edition 2023

Written by Linda Pistun
Illustrated by Candice Ossman
Book design and Edited by Tabletop Publishing

ISBN: 978-1-960638-17-5 (paperback)
ISBN: 978-1-960638-16-8 (hardback)
Ebook: 978-1-960638-18-2

Library of Congress Control Number: 2023939975

Published by Tabletop Publishing
Tabletop Teaching Limited Liability Company
4030 Wake Forest Road STE 349
Raleigh, NC 27609

TABLETOP
PUBLISHING

This book is for my Mom, Katie Pistun, who taught me to make mistakes, and who always had a hug or a book when I needed it.

And for my Kindergarten teacher, Michelle Koob, who always saw me as a scientist - with or without front teeth.

And finally, this book is for all the little girls with big dreams.

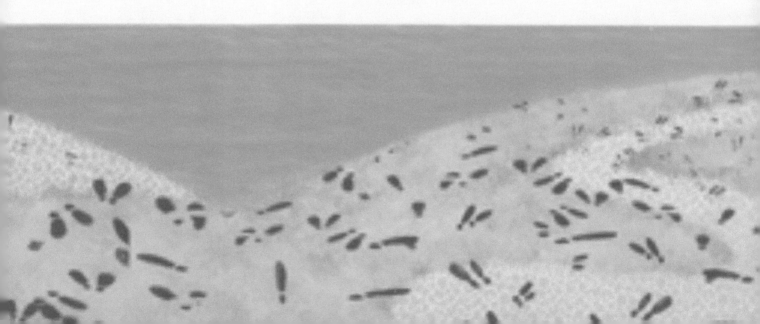

LINDA AND THE MYSTERIOUS FOOTPRINTS

Written by
Linda Pistun

Illustrated by
Candice Ossman

"Sunny day, here I come!" Linda shouted as she looked out at the **beautiful**, **bright** sky, "I am OUT of here!"

After working in her lab all morning, it was time for a break. Linda put on her hiking boots and settled her pet turtle into his carrier.

"Let's go, Darwin," she said. "It's time for a hike in the forest."

2

As they traveled down the road toward the forest, Linda noticed that the **familiar**, **old** sign didn't look quite the same. She parked her bike and walked over to take a closer **peek**. "**Darwin**, there's something strange going on here. These marks look like… **footprints**!"

As they **gazed** ahead, where the forest **used to be**—
there were no trees.

"This just can't be!" Linda said, "Where are the trees?"
Instead of trees, black **footprints** covered the ground.

Linda was **confused**. What was *happening?*
She grabbed **Darwin**, **hopped** on her bike, and **raced**
back to her **lab**. It was time to do some **research**.

Linda **Googled** everything she could think of to find out what happened to the forest.

"Oh, no!" she said to **Darwin**, "People **cut down** the trees to make room for more houses. Our **beautiful forest** is gone!"

From her window, Linda looked out at her neighbor's **farm**, "What!?" she exclaimed, grabbing her **binoculars**. The cows were covered with black **footprints**!

"Why didn't I notice this before? Where else will we find these **footprints**?"

Even **Darwin** looked confused.

Linda was curious. Now she wondered
if the **ocean** still looked the same.

"Dad, can we take a **ride** to the beach?" she asked.
"Sure," her dad said. "Let's pack a **picnic** and go **boating**."
As they drifted away from the dock, they saw black
footprints all over the **ocean**!

The next day, as Linda walked through town, there they were again—black **footprints** all over **houses**... and even **cars**!

Linda gasped, "**Black footprints** are EVERYWHERE! I need to stop this." Linda's dad gave her a big hug. "Thanks, Dad."

Linda knew what she needed to do next.

"**Darwin**, we have to go talk to the Mayor about these **strange footprints**," said Linda.

"Mr. Dosey," Linda showed the Mayor a photo on her phone, "we need your **help**. We have to find out who made these **footprints**."

13

"Oh! I agree!" said Mayor Dosey, "We can use the town hall **computers** to do the **research**."

Linda and Mayor Dosey agreed that they would use the **Scientific Method** to find the answer.

LINDA USES THE SCIENTIFIC METHOD

STEP 2:
RESEARCH
Use all your **resources** to find out more.

STEP 1:
ASK A QUESTION
"What are the **footprints** made of?"

16

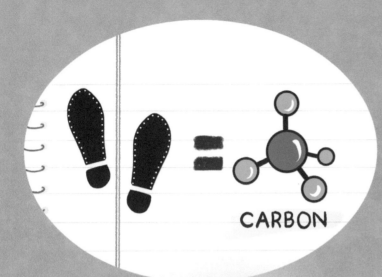

CARBON

STEP 3:
FORM A HYPOTHESIS
The footprints are made of **carbon**.

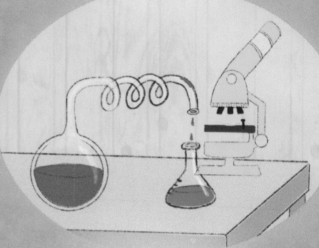

STEP 4:
EXPERIMENT
Test a footprint **sample**.

6
C
Carbon
12.011

STEP 5:
CONCLUSION
The footprints are **CARBON**!

Linda and Mayor Dosey decided to fix the **carbon footprints** in their town. They invited everyone to a town meeting. "Welcome," said Mayor Dosey, "this is an important meeting. Linda, our young **scientist**, will explain why you are seeing black **footprints** everywhere."

What is YOUR Carbon Footprint?

Linda stepped up to the microphone, "**Carbon dioxide** is created whenever we use **fossil fuels**. Driving a car, turning on lights, raising animals for food, and not recycling trash are all ways we produce more **carbon dioxide**. The more we use **fossil fuels**, the more **carbon dioxide** is created. This is called a **carbon footprint**. It is our **negative impact** on the **Earth**."

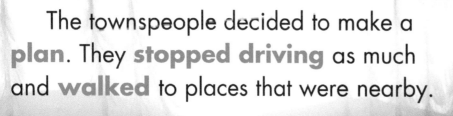

The townspeople decided to make a **plan**. They **stopped driving** as much and **walked** to places that were nearby.

They turned **lights off** if they didn't need them. The farmer even **stopped raising cows** and grew **food crops** instead.

The townspeople went to the forest. Together, they planted **hundreds of baby trees** and made a promise to **nurture** them and let them **grow**.

They posted **signs** so other people would know not to cut down the **trees**.

Pretty Please
Don't cut down the trees! 2♥

They also posted **signs** at the beach,
reminding people not to throw **trash** in the ocean.

The **carbon footprints** soon became
smaller
and
smaller.

And as their **footprints** got smaller, the trees grew taller, and the air and ocean became **cleaner**.

Soon the **carbon footprints** were so small that nobody could see them.

As a special gift, Mayor Dosey gave Linda a key to the city for helping save the **environment**. Linda and Darwin were so proud!

MESSAGES IN THIS STORY

- Everything we do impacts our environment either in a positive or negative way
- It's up to us to work together as a community to reduce our carbon footprint
- There are several ways to reduce our carbon footprint
- Teamwork can achieve the most difficult feats
- You don't have to be an adult to make a difference
- Anyone is capable of doing great things

THINGS TO TALK ABOUT

- How can we reduce our carbon footprint?
- What ways did Linda help the town?
- Do you have to be grown up to help the environment?
- What ways can you help your community?
- What do you already do to reduce your carbon footprint?

WAYS TO REDUCE

Use electric vehicles.

Bike or walk more.

Eat less meat.

Plant trees.

Wash in COLD water.

Reduce, Reuse, & Recycle.

YOUR CARBON FOOTPRINT

MAKE YOUR OWN PLAN

What will you and your loved ones do to reduce
your carbon footprint at home?

Ask a Question	
Research your Question	
Form a Hypothesis	
Perform an Experiment	
Conclusion	

COMPOSTING IN 7 EASY STEPS

Darwin thanks you!
(Yes, he's a real turtle.)

1. Choose the type of compost bin for your backyard.

2. Choose the location of your composter.

3. Alternate layers.

4. Keep adding kitchen and yard waste as they accumulate.

5. Repeat until your bin is full.

6. Take care of your compost bin.

7. Collect your compost.

COMPOST

FOR MORE ACTIVITIES SCAN THE QR CODE BELOW

LOVE THE BOOK? TRY THIS SPECIAL VIDEO BOOK VERSION OF "LINDA AND THE MYSTERIOUS FOOTPRINTS". SCAN TO START WATCHING!

ABOUT THE AUTHOR

Linda Pistun is an entrepreneur, writer, and scientist living in Northern Virginia. She shares her laboratory with her box turtle, Darwin. Linda was five years old when she discovered her passion for math and science. She knew she wanted to make a difference in the world, and a tank of mealworms gave her the perfect idea.

Linda opened Linda's Lab in 2017, with two big goals. She wanted to solve world hunger through mealworm protein and improve science education for girls like her. Through the Larva Library, Linda's Lab loans mealworm tanks to local classrooms, giving others the chance to experience and be inspired by science.

Linda wrote "Linda and the Mysterious Footprints" to inspire young kids like herself to follow their passions. She also wanted to show the world that pigtails and lab coats DO go together!

Follow Linda on social media: @LindasLab

IF YOU LIKED THIS BOOK...

Check out our other children's books, merch, and literacy journals by scanning the QR code.

Or visit www.TabletopTeachingLLC.com

TABLETOP
PUBLISHING

FOLLOW US ON SOCIAL MEDIA

CUSTOMIZE YOUR BOOK

Use the blank pages at the back of this book to write about, draw, and explore your personal passion. Enjoy making this book as unique as you! Have fun and keep learning.

Printed in the USA
CPSIA information can be obtained
at www.ICGtesting.com
LVHW060922131223
765943LV00072B/724